THE CREMATE BURY TALES

The Crematebury Tales
by Meeta Khanna
Paperback Edition

First Published in 2023 by

Inkfeathers Publishing
Vivek Vihar, New Delhi 110095
www.inkfeathers.com

ISBN 978-81-960895-5-9

THE CREMATE BURY TALES

MEETA KHANNA

Inkfeathers Publishing
www.inkfeathers.com

Dedicated to those who need to read this,

but will not read this,

even though they need to read this.

CONTENTS

PREFACE

A journey can be a metaphor for life. Life can be a metaphor for a journey. Both may not be metaphorical.

A home or a bus is but a microcosm of the world. It will have its own laws. Laws are to be abided by or be broken.

The world is always changing. Change can be a threat or a challenge. Both require a response.

Every life is a story by itself. Every story has a life of its own. Both have a potential to be mundane or phenomenal.

The storyteller has a perspective. The reader has another. The uniqueness of each enriches the narrative.

Every story brings learning. The learning can be desirable or undesirable. However, it can be rejected or accepted, both carry a separate value.

Ignorance is not bliss. Bliss may be a side effect of ignorance. The corollary is also true.

Reading makes an individual think. Thinking is potentially harmful to complacency. Do not read.

The fabric of life is woven with the warp of intellect, the weft of emotions on the physical loom of actions. All three exist in harmony.

Harmony is a prerequisite. A prerequisite to anything, anything and everything. Even chaos. It can be the outcome too, though that is not guaranteed.

All is preordained. Everything is random. The random may be pre-ordained or the pre-ordained may be random.

Those who experience life, learn from their experiences. Those who fear the experience of life, learn from their fear. The respective learnings are diverse.

But not always.

Love is a by-product of imagination. The more vivid the imagination, the more powerful the experience. Keep your imagination in check.

One may imagine many worlds. One may reimagine this world. A world may exist in imagination alone but be true, for imagination is also a component of truth.

Each individual may perceive a unique aspect of truth. A diamond may have many facets. All are real.

The reader of a story is a character too. Though they exist outside the story, they shape the frame of reference. That alone decides the interpretation, the outcome and the value assigned to it.

The study of literature is the study of everything and everyone. A student of literature requires many lifetimes to encompass its entirety. It may still not be accomplished.

"Life is short. Art long. Opportunity is fleeting.

Experience treacherous. Judgement difficult."

Geoffrey Chaucer has already said all that can be said and told all the tales that can be told.

All that we are left with is example and inspiration.

I dedicate this piece of writing to that example and inspiration.

We must always begin as we mean to go on.
To do anything else results in a surprise.
Surprises are sometimes shocks.
But not always.

PROLOGUE

I am Massimo Pilot, driven by my circumstances to drive you to your destination. The expressway is beyond description and defeats imagination. I am smarter than you know, crazier than I show, I have been told a lot of things, big and small, I keep them to myself, never tell all. This will be a ride that you won't forget, listen, learn, enjoy, don't worry, don't fret.

For I know the way.

The summer sun sat smiling in the sultry summer sky, not partaking in the random worries of all and sundry, the year was half gone and had been a tough ride, some of us had lost our jobs, some had lost our wives, some of us had lost our health, some of us, our lives.

The dastardly disease was dastardly and deadly, to tell the truth, it struck at our lungs, it struck at our breath, if it went away, it did; if it did not go, it was a major cause of death.

This year the doctors had worked more than they ever had, the nurses had had it even tougher, but the gravediggers had it really bad.

Round the clock the fires burnt in pyres in and out of

cremation mounds, far and widespread the flames and reached the burial grounds.

The gravediggers spent all day digging the graves and burying the piling dead, they shook their heads in ancient wisdom wondering as to whatever lay ahead.

I sat in the driver's seat, the bus was ready for the road, Oldtimes Hospital had run out of doses, there were twenty-nine citizens left still unbestowed.

We would leave for the Crisper Facility a hundred miles away, to get for all, the latest possible jabs in the latest possible way. We had the tech, we had the AI and even AI's bots, however somehow, we had run out of required vaccine shots.

One by one, piled in the bus, in spirits high and fine, the varied passengers, a total of twenty-nine. I said to each as they clambered on, it is a long drive and I should stay awake, tell me your story as we go, for true companionship's sake.

When we stop at the pub for a short break, whoever tells the best story, an opinion poll we'll take.

So, if you do, your drink's on me.

"Yes, the meal is free!"

They laughed behind their masks and high fived the air, for it was a good deal meant to be fair, a fine story for a finer wine and the finest meal there.

The first one to get on, get in, get to his seat was a great (gentle) man, rotund and stout, warm and loud,

The honourable MP was full of accomplishment.

Education, diplomacy, social work and a long stint in the Parliament. He smiled at everyone, the epitome of a soul benevolent.

Accompanied by his PA, a deliberate charmer most oily, with slicked back hair, a slicked over smile, a slick snake like style, He checked his phone regularly, the device must cost my year's worth of salary.

There were two men with all the trappings of wealth, they spoke to each other about their financial health. The Industrialist and the Stockbroker, their caste was money, their creed was power. Deep in discussion, their laptops' screen had all their attention. They did not look at the others or speak or hear, they spoke of the bullion and the bull and the bear.

There was a woman of a certain age, with a face of stone and a barely suppressed groan, a bagful of bag under each eye, a frown and an uncertain sad sigh. Dressed in the colour of mud, a dull drab brown, she looked tired, weary and let down, by all the world and the heavens too, she sat alone in a corner, wearing brown and feeling blue. She had run a bookstore, once thriving and stand alone, now run down, thus her face of stone.

There was also a Man of God. He spent equal time reading, sleeping, eating and drinking. He seemed to be a most contained and contented person, who seemed asleep, but could possibly be thinking.

A man of scrubs, fortune's favours, fortune's rubs. To be a doctor in times like these, not a moment of well-being, not a moment of peace, not a moment of comfort, not a moment of ease. Pain, and only pain had been brought by the Pandemic, he had thought to classify pain as endemic. He stared out of the window, wherever was he, he didn't seem to know.

The pharmacist, tired of face and tired from days, sitting tiredly he tirelessly stared in space. He looked the antonym of cheery, exhausted and grey, extremely weary, had suffered through the longest week of longer days, of tough times and suffering ways, a pharmacist of some repute and diligence, he sat aloof with some elegance.

One sat slumped with a lost air of hopeless striving, this year, it was ambulances he had been driving.

There was one apple among men, apples bloomed in his rosy cheeks, apples in his middle, he laughed, he smiled, he joked, he grinned, fit as a fiddle.

A friendly one, with a ready smile on offer, he was growing as a grocer. Apples, bananas, celery, he shared freely, his ABC of grocery.

There was one frail and sweet yet looked as if made of steel, a young woman with spectacles perching on her nose, or head and forgotten for a while, dressed simply, with an infectious grin that would make you smile. She helped me assign seats to everyone and helped in distribution of care kits and specified the 'do's and 'don'ts with charm and wit. An elementary school teacher and a pretty one at that, she said she is okay, but missed her pet cat. Her cat must miss her more, of that I am quite sure.

Designer hair, tinted just the in shade of gold and highlights of pink, designer shades, a bespoke dress and eye-catching ink, muscles in right places, curves in correct detail, the two actors sauntered in, everyone else in comparison paled to a pale shade of pale. The duo magnifico were too magnificent to be real, and I began to believe in the magnificence of the reel. She just had to smile at me, and I began to reel.

A glamorous being joined them, too dazzling, too tall, too everything, a model on and off the ramp, she joined the Duo Magnifico's camp.

The undergraduate looked at her once, he did not look away, his underdeveloped prefrontal cortex quite on display. He flexed his triceps and stuck out his chest, he deepened his voice, and showed off at his best.

The Professor cocked a curious eyebrow above a sardonic look and immediately whipped out an impressive book, adjusted her earplugs, looking at us as if we were ignorant bugs, we were minor species to her mighty brain, or she was already in her own orbit, and we were somewhat sane.

There was one nouveau riche and full of vulgar talk, he had a maligning nature and a swaggering walk. He thought that he was just too cool. An entrepreneur, he called himself, a million masks sold in a week! What cheek! A braggart and a fool.

The sailor was a man who cheated fate, yet felt cheated by fate, he seemed sick of life as he sat thinking of his probably, possibly most probably, cheating wife.

The Software Guy was sweet and kind, the milk of human kindness overflowing. "What can I do to help you?" Ah! Your generosity is showing.

His wife, a Lawyer, did not sympathize with human need. She was full of gluttony and full of greed.

A middle-aged man full of charm and joy, handsome as a rock idol, effervescent as a boy, in love with love and light, a poet by day, a bartender by night. His partner was a sweetheart, and that set him apart.

And one who said nothing and did nothing, a woman of dubious intentions, for her supper, she said, she would sing, but I thought her lack of music suspect. She said, 'Yeah! Fact!'

There was one who was a bringer of bad tidings, saying that he spoke the truth, based on facts and findings, a news anchor, as false as false can be, for false is what they know and false is all they speak, anything for a TRP, or currying favour with the current flavour, in their political life, or sleeping with the enemy's wife.

There was a punk rock band. They called themselves FourForFour, they were Primo, the long-haired lead vocalist, Twain, the much-tattooed drummer, Tressa, the orange flame of the forest hair vocalist and lead guitarist, and the goth Ivy, with her keyboard. They occupied the last seat and remained in their own zone, with rhythm and lyrics and each a headphone.

The last one in was a man who had to carry everyone's load and sorrow, who dug graves for a living and could not believe in a tomorrow, whose hope was gone, he felt all alone, and cried for those who had gone.

I greeted all with hospitality and grace. At treating clients perfectly, I am an unbeatable ace. Having worked for five years in a hotel well placed, it was the downturn in the tourism sector that had me thus displaced. I could have been rolling in tips and appreciation, here I am driving this most unremarkable busload to their vaccination.

I asked the first seated to begin with his tale. His was expected to be large in implication, large as his scale.

The rule of people and the rule of kings

both leave much to be desired.

That is also a law of progress.

1.

The MP's Tale

The hon'ble MP, honourably named Dave, honourably got up from his seat, honourably waved at all afore, honourably smiled and nodded, he smiled and waved some more.

"Greetings to all gathered here. I am with you, my friends, my fellow sufferers, I am with you. We are all in this together. I am with you. We are all in this together." He looked at everyone, his honourable benevolence fell from him like rain, he moved his hands, as if to take away our collective pain.

The PA looked at his face with awe, spoke in hushed tones and with folded hands, "He is a Great Man."

The Great Man smiled nodding at everyone, his pumpkin-like face glowed orange in the light of the afternoon sun. He continued in similar cause, "We are all together in this. And we will win this fight." He waited for applause. The band screamed from the back, "A story! A story! We want a story." The great man smiled benevolently, and he said,

"There was once an ant hill, it was on the top of a hill. The ants went downhill, the ants went uphill. They worked all summer; they ate all winter.

They worked hard, the ants must work hard, whether it's democracy or not, unless the ants work hard, a nation's effort comes to nought.

They had a chosen leader. Chosen, yet a queen, a winner.

I appeal to all of you gathered here. People! Choose your leader with wisdom and skill, show your citizenship and political will.

Then follow your chosen leader. An ant you must always be, that will keep you fulfilled and happy! And busy! For that is necessary."

He smiled at everyone around once more, then reclined his seat, settled down to snore. Well, if I had wanted a speech, I would have asked for one, but I had wanted a story from that honourable old bore.

His PA slid sideways to the driver's seat to speak softly in my ear, to insinuate that if I wanted the Great Man to say something providing inspiration, the PA must be spoken to, in advance, with an advance, unless the party was campaigning for election.

I said, thanks but no, not required, at this stage in my life, I could barely tolerate being inspired. The PA hissed, "But I can tell you many stories. I can because I know People, and People know me. I ask you to come to my city. You will know who Spoonerwala is, they know me as the man who knows people and who can get things done. That's who I am! I can get things done."

A human being is an infinite being.

With infinite possibilities, infinite futures,

infinite in their dreams, wisdom,

and achievement.

A sycophant is a human being too.

II.

The PA's Tale

In his oily voice, he began to speak with an ingratiating smile, trying to look humble, achieving a look supremely servile.

He bowed his head towards the Great Man, nodding his head.

He said, "He is a Great Man. Even in his childhood, he was a Great Man. Who am I? I am nobody."

He shook his head from side to side as if dancing on a snake charmer's pipe. A Nobody. But I know People. Yes. I know People. And People know me. And People know that I know People." He smiled; his smile coupled with that cunning eye made me think of a reptile. A slithery, slimy snake sliding through the sliding possibilities of his public life. He hissed, "I can get things done. In my city. If you ever come to my city and you need things done, well, here is my calling card. Spoonerwala, at your service." He pulled out a silver case from one of many of his pockets, handing one each to everyone. Once last year, there was an acute shortage." He lowered his sibilance even further. "The medicine for the disease, it just was not available. Even he could not get it." He gestured towards the good doctor.

"Someone needed it. It was a matter of life and death. Life and Death. Yes. He requested, Please Spooney Sir. I said No Problem. I made a call. I know People. You can get anything done, in my city, but you must know People. And you can get anything for a Price."

He smiled with a feigned benevolence at all of us. His eyes met mine, in the rear-view, there was no smile in his eyes. I braked suddenly.

He stopped sullenly, mid strike, but continued without breaking his stride.

"Now he is a Great Man. His heart is for his people. I was a Nobody. But he trusts me like his son."

The Great Man did not look as if he had a son, or he knew how to trust one had he had one.

"I was sixteen, in a small town, with nothing to do, nowhere to go. He had come on a tour; his car broke down. There was just one car in the whole of our slow and sleepy town, it belonged to my cranky old uncle, the crank refused without even listening to me, I cranked the crank's arm, and ran off with the key."

He spoke of his misdeed with an uncommon sense of pride.

"From that day, I never moved from the Great Man's side.

When he rose, I rose, when he fell, I held on for the ride.

He said Spooney. Stay with me, you can get things done. Not someone to be side lined, I can get things done. I know

People."

I did not want to listen to his litany of deeds to which he aspired. I wondered about the Crank's arm, and what had truly transpired?

I turned to the two glued to the laptop screen, concentration subtext, the industrialist and the stockbroker, waving me off to the next. "Later." They spoke together, "Later."

The human race is motivated to do many things. The motivation itself arises out of factors which are as random as they are specific. Earning a great deal of money even at the cost of human disaster in the times of human catastrophe has been seen to happen many times and will be seen again till the end of the time.

However unsettling this may be, this remains a fact of human existence.

Though philanthropy exists.

A coin has two faces, a human being has many.

III.

The Mask Maker's Tale

"Let me tell you a few things, and I know what I am talking about, like really. I am Mr Opar Chewn, the owner of Best Enterprises, it's a private company. You must have heard of me. I have been trending lately. On social media and all. I have millions of followers and all."

Loud. Voice. Tone. Even the colour of his branded clothes, all imitation. All loud. "I am self-made." I imagined his immaculate birth as he basked in his own sense of worth. "I had some premises, a shop, at the beginning of the year, then I began my enterprises."

He was too colourful, too loud, too vociferous, too everything to be ignored, and as it is everyone was just a wee bit bored.

"I put my wife on the machines."

This had my imagination in an overdrive, dramatic and mean, before from his words, his meaning I could glean.

"We were into masks. She made them. I sold them. Then I got five girls more. Regular factory like it was. Then I rented the next-door garage. It had no work going. Got the boys on to filling the oxygen cylinders. Meanwhile, I bought oximeters. Quite cheap. Sold them. Made a packet on that. Demand and supply, that's that."

The doctor was listening with unwavering attention too. "Then came the real breakthrough. Got a mega order for the vile disease testing kits! Though the disease did not prove to be vile, speaking for myself! That was huge, the testing kits. I worked hard, but I used my brain and took my chance."

"Did you exercise any quality control checks?" The doctor seemed to have taken an aggressive stance.

"Who has the time for such nonsense?"

"Do you know the number of people who we lost to it, the faulty oxygen cylinders and the cost of your profit?"

"What could I do under the circumstances?"

The good doctor jumped from his seat, streaked through the aisle, screamed "Murderer," holding him by his collar.

"I am an entrepreneur."

I guess accrued profit was his situational benefit.

"Peace, folks. Stay calm." I had to intervene.

"Murderer!" muttered the doctor, sinking back into his apathy and seemed dazed.

Mr. Chewn glared daggers but remained unfazed.

"Some people cannot bear other people's success."

"Pit-stop break." It was time to stop the fight.

"Sandwiches, coffee, juice, or a light."

Nature is supreme.

Though man disagrees.

And continues to battle nature.

This battle will be decisive.

For everyone.

IV.

The Professor's Tale

"Good day everyone. I am Geena. Let me tell you the parable of the beast," spoke the professor in her best lecture-room tone; even the self-made man looked up from his phone.

"Once upon a time, a powerful oriental king
sent his twenty best knights to go hunting.
They returned with a beast, ferocious and wild.
The beast killed all, man, woman and child.
It would not be tamed, it broke captivity.
Devastating the land, traveling by air and sea.
It could not be described; it could not be held.
For the king and the kingdom, doom it spelled.
The king asked his knights to let it roam
wherever it desired, away from his lands and home.
The beast grew powerful and stronger,

captivated, coaxed and controlled no longer.
It could kill, maim, murder by suffocation.
There was no one to stop its evolution.
Nations fell while it held the world at ransom.
An omnipresent one, it slaughtered at random.
The fear grew, the deaths upscaled.
The fevers grew, the cures failed.
Slowly the populations gathered their forces,
pitted their brains, pooled their resources.
Slowly and slowly things improved.
By this time, the beast had proved,
there is much that we do not know.
Arrogance that we do goes to show,
this universe has much hidden still.
Nature's secrets, supremacy and will.
We must live with respect for the living.
Many came forward, compassionate and giving.
The beast taught us how to survive,
only till the next breath that we are alive.
To conquer all, unbound ambition is a sin.
The universe is vaster than you can win.
The king in the castle, the knights in grave.
The beast still lives, we need to be brave.
A collective battle, a collected thought.
With patience and knowledge, it will be caught.

A lesson should be learned to last us awhile.

The dead must be remembered, lest we dare to smile."

She regained her seat, boarded the bus,

leaving us pondering, the ignorance of us.

The stone-faced woman, lost in her misery, stumbled.

Suddenly, tears in flood, her stony face crumbled.

"The dead must be remembered," whispered she. That was before she broke down completely.

The dead must be remembered.

The lessons must be learned.

Immediately.

Otherwise, both may grow exponentially.

V.

The Bookseller's Tale

"It was all because of me. I continued to open the store, as it is we were not doing well before. I got it. I thought I was hale, hearty and strong. I did not even think twice that I could be wrong. It was all my fault. All my doing or rather my wrongdoing. I was casual about it all. Sometimes we do not look at the large picture. We have opinions, we have points of view, we trade in our half knowledge and consider it to be all knowledge."

Her rising voice was a lament, her eyes a pool of misery, it did not seem that she would smile ever again. Vanquished by her agony, she was an ocean of pain.

"My father had sold all his ancestral land. It was his dream to open a little Book Store at the corner of the street. This had always been his dream. My mother was an avid reader. She stumbled across this little Book Store. It was love at first sight. She would step in almost every day to browse or to enquire about new books. Sometimes she would order a new publication. My father, a young man half in love with the idea of love, fell in love with this girl who was already in love with the idea of love. The books they shared and constantly talked about led them to talk about anything and everything in the world and all that is out of this world. Their love bloomed with the bookstore and flourished with it. This marriage was made in heaven and was only carried out on earth. My mother shared his dream and loved it too. My mother and father had written their love story in the shape of a bookstore in a small town when they were very young. Theirs' is a love story. It was a love story as long as they lived. Their greatest joy was getting up in the morning and going to open that bookstore. Their greatest plans were plans for buying old and new books for their store. My sister was a book lover and a romantic too. Simple people, happy lives. All lost! All lost to the dastardly disease."

She broke off in the middle of a sentence.

She looked broken as if she was going through a sentence.

"The infection. I was asymptomatic. I had never been ever sick, a single day of my life. yet I carried the disease home with me. It was an octopus with uncountable arms. It was a monster that grew and grew as it fed on everything I loved. It fed and it grew larger. I lost my father. I lost my mother. My sister, my brother. They were all in the hospital. Then the medical bills arrived. I had to sell the store. They did not survive. I have lost their store."

"I thought I was Invincible.

Here I am invincible."

She sobbed uncontrollably.

"It was all I had. My family. The store. We lived above. It

had been in my family for more than three decades. No more."

She slumped where she sat. Her grief was all she was left with. She had lost all her lifelines. Now she was at sea, all alone.

"I don't know what to do anymore. My father, my mother, my sister, and my brother. All my life. Their store. Now there is just the silence and pain. And endless bills, unpaid. We must remember the dead."

She fell silent. There was no story in her except one of the human predicament that we all found ourselves in. Sometimes the only stories we have are our stories of sadness of loss and of pain. Maybe nobody wants to hear them because they make the listener forgo their own joy and search for empathy in the dark depths of their own soul.

Sometimes the listener is willing to give the gift of empathy and silence, sometimes their own life is too difficult, and they have their own sorrow to carry with them wherever they go.

Her sorrow fell on us like a shroud of silence.

This silence was broken by the shrug of an expressive shoulder.

The long legs strode through the length of the aisle.

"Let me tell you about my dead."

The model had a fascinating husky voice, frothy like foam, sparkling like wine, which sent frissons of awareness up and down my spine.

Love.

It takes us places, at times.

At times, it takes us.

VI.

The Model's Tale

"I am Alisa. You can call me Ali or Lisa or A. This is about six months back. My BAE had a touch of the lazies, asked me to get him some rolls of tissue, he had run out of them. I didn't want to go, but I did, 'cause I didn't want to create an issue. Well, I caught the flu and gave it to him too. I got better, he got worse, off to the hospital and the ICU. His boss came over to comfort me, he comforted me a bit too much, he caught it too. It wasn't your regular flu."

She smiled a gap-toothed smile, took a sip of her wine, studied it for a while.

"He shouldn't have asked me to go to the mart when I didn't want to go! I couldn't think of going back home, so much stress, and so I went to my ex's. He took a look at my face, he figured he had missed me, so passionately he kissed me. One thing just led to another, and another to bed. I said NO! He thought I would want to, but I didn't! Well, the stupid oaf should have listened. It was the ICU for him too."

She paused and lifted her lush blonde hair a bit away from

her slender neck, shook them back, and they cascaded down her back.

"So, Tuesday my test result said, I was positive. The next three days! Terrible! Wednesday my BAE, Thursday, his boss, Friday, my ex! One, two, three! I was like crazy. I needed to talk to someone, I went to this pub near me. There was this guy, his eyes were full of empathy. He came over so that I could sleep. I had been feeling things way too deep."

We shook our heads in sympathy.

"What happened to him, Ali?"

"Who? That one? He caught it badly, probably from me. I am not someone who makes a good lonesome, I can only be one half of a twosome."

"He died a week to a day. And my husband who I had been planning to divorce had already passed away."

This was a silence of a different stature.

Her soft eyes and luscious lips spoke of her loving nature as she began her tale.

"Here is a story I liked much. Carlos was an impulsive young man, driven by his youth and impulse, he would fall in love at the drop of a hat and fall out as fast again. The intermittent period was a roller coaster ride. Once walking by the city forest near the old cemetery, he happened to catch a glimpse of a woman walking at a distance. She seemed alluring and more attractive than any woman he had ever met before. He asked her to stay and chat, she would not stay. He asked her to tell him her name, she refused. He ran after her and, impulsive as he was, attempted to detain her by holding her hand.

He said, 'Listen to me please. I am completely floored by your charm and beauty. I love you. I shall love you as long as I can, I shall love you forever and beyond. I shall love you till eternity. I love you with everything I possess, all my hopes, all my dreams, all my songs.'

She warned him not to. 'Tell me your name.' He implored her to.

'Stay with me. Don't leave me. I shall miss you the moment you are gone. Do not forsake me, do not leave me alone. I shall be alone if you are gone. I shall be lonely. I want to be with you. I want to be with you today. I want to be with you tomorrow. I want to be with you forever. Stay with me. Be mine.'

Carlos was passionate. Carlos was ardent. He would not let her go.

This moment was his only reality, he was true, it wasn't just for show.

This is how he was, whenever he fell in love, he really fell in love.

He whispered.

'My love! Stay with me. Take my heart, take my hand, take my soul.

She asked him to leave. He sat down on a headstone. She asked him to be silent. He began to sing a love song. She asked him to not call her by any name once she began walking away from him.

He called out to her, 'I am Carlos, and you are Carla.'

She stopped and asked him, 'What do you wish for?'

Carlos, the impulsive youth that he was, spoke with passion, “I want you to kiss me and be with me always.’

‘Always?’

‘Always.’

She kissed him and both of them disappeared forever.

Forever.

Carlos was never seen again. The headstone was engraved with the legend, “Here lies Carla, young and pretty, who died in search of her one true love.”

Ali was quiet for a moment.

“He shouldn’t have asked me to go to the mart. One must let a woman follow her wishes. In everything.”

“Like Carlos!”

Another sip of wine, she sauntered back sensual and slow, sitting down next to the undergraduate, who began to emit a hormonal glow.

I was a bit scared after this story. I asked Tara, the elementary school teacher if she would share a story.

Women, ancient souls, ageless bodies,
flowing limbs

holding hands across the seas, the lands,
the boundaries

a circle of love, strong hearts, bathed in
a golden glow,

moving in out of moment in time, creating a
bridge out of fragments of life, holding each
other up, shelter from storms

a lake in reflection, a river in flow, a pond at
peace, the surface at rest.

Do not throw a stone, or even a pebble.

Beware, you have been warned.

VII.

The Elementary School Teacher's Tale

She took a sip from her cup and spoke softly.

"I know many stories, I have been telling them all year, sometimes they teach a value, sometimes soothe a fear. My kids are very young, all teaching was online, initially it was tough, later it was fine. We unlearned a few things, learned some new, relearned everything anew. My kids (there are eighteen of them) taught me a lot, especially one, little Tom, his parents always fought. Once during a lesson, he just wouldn't turn his video on, it took a lot of persuasion to even turn his audio on. When he did, there was a tremor in his voice, and in the background, there was an indistinct muffled noise. I was alert to all situations, asked him some leading questions. I began to play an action word game; they would have to perform the specified action when I called their name. Little Tom, I asked him to make a silly face, that sinister blue-black bruise he displayed was a disgrace. Later I made a call, he told me all. How can a father mature and grown, be so violent towards a child, that too his own? I brought a counsellor in, she helped him. His mother was bruised, broken, scared and battered, such terrible violence, a family shattered."

"But I don't want to tell you little Tom's story, I want to tell you my grandmother's story. She was very old."

"It was long ago, my grandmother sat in her backyard, grinding some corn on an old-fashioned grinding stone. She was a woman soft and kind, my grandfather was a domineering man with a stubborn mind. He would dictate to her, and she would accede to, his demands and wishes she agreed to.

Many came to her kitchen to be fed, the homeless, the poor, those in need, they were never denied. That day, one homeless person in the neighbourhood, who sold some goods to earn a livelihood, burning with fever asked for food.

My grandfather, whose middle name must have been Sir Extremely Prudent Almost a Miser, grumbled somewhat about the rising cost of living. My grandmother gave him the coldest of the cold look, unforgettable and absolutely unforgiving.

She gestured to her corn or her grinding stone, said to him in a coldest of the cold tone, one word more and I shall throw this on your head, in my kitchen the hungry will be fed. My grandfather slunk to his room, for many days sunk in gloom.

I, to this day, do not know if she meant the corn or the stone, a woman made of silk, with steel for her backbone.

My grandmother sat me down and said to me, "We can

agree, and we can disagree, we can speak up, we can speak out, a woman is always her own mistress, in spirit free."

Tara sat contemplating her coffee.

I had a thought but kept my peace.

Not a gender issue, everyone is free. Or ought to be.

Liberty, freedom and respect are intertwined.

Travel whenever you can. You will learn how.

But only if you are ready to learn.

VIII.

The Bartender's Tale

Once upon a time, a crab family lived in a rock pool by the sea.

The baby crab asked his parents if he could go out of the pool to see the world. The mother began to cry, the father shouted at him to not be a fool, there is nothing outside the pool.

The baby crab spoke to them nicely, crying and shouting are no solutions to any problem, we must discuss things properly.

So, he went a-roaming, a-looking, He saw the beach, sand and sun, he saw families having fun. He told them about the world so, there are many things to see and know.

Once he saw a man and a crab, the crab was cooked and was food. He came back and said that though we are all free, our freedom must ensure everyone's liberty.

Once he saw many crabs in a bucket, pulling each other down, not a single crab could get out and be free. He told everyone that teamwork is the key, a law-abiding supportive community ensures freedom and liberty. If everyone is free, then all are free.

Once this crab walked into the bar and slapped down a bill, he said he had time to kill, and invited me to chill. Beer, he wanted, he observed thus and said, thus. Pouring the beer is also an art and essential for offering at the best bars. The glass should be held at 45-degree angle, and you should aim it towards the middle of the glass slope. When the glass is 2/3 full then pour it at 90 degrees angle, and below 10 degrees C, that's the correct temperature for me.

I wondered if crabs drank beer, was it usual? He responded easily, saying that freedom depends on a basic principle, leave it to the individual."

The bartender smiled affably; his partner applauded enthusiastically.

"It was a beautiful story, but then all your stories are always divine, let me tell you mine."

If we can rid the world of one thing,

just one,

let it be prejudice.

All prejudice.

IX.

The Partner's Tale

"Call me Benny."

Consider a small town, with nowhere to go, nothing to do. Visualize a young boy, unlike his father and brother, living in a world of stereotypes, not believing in them, living and dreaming of living a very different life.

Imagine a family entrenched in conforming to a concept, a life perfect. But nothing remains perfect. Things change when young boys grow into young men."

This young man was poetic, artistic, fond of music and dance, and most decidedly interested in other young men in matters of love and romance.

His family was aghast and shocked. They wanted him put away and locked. At least till he was over this and cured. Never, he told them, be assured. Things were uglier than they can be described. He was beaten and bullied; strange cures prescribed.

Beaten. Beaten black and blue. Just because he wanted to be himself, just because he did not feel the way you do or think like you? He began to retreat within, hollow cheeked, skeletal thin."

Shadows were dark falling on us like black and blue bruises, we were all feeling the weight of his loneliness. "Then there was a wedding. A homegrown movie star was coming back home to be married, and who was tending the bar? Our Russo!

Love at the first cocktail."

Benny laughed. He threw back his head and laughed in sheer exuberance of love and simple delight. The shadows vanished, leaving us in light.

We realized he had shared his own story with us.

We had come part of the way, but there are still many miles to go.

Everyone seemed somewhat inclined towards sleep, but we were alert to this beautiful diction in a baritone deep. It was the actor, theatrical and commanding.

Destiny is strange.

You may not believe in it.

You may not find it.

It may believe in you and find you.

The outcome is always the same.

X.

The Actor's Tale

"A little boy dreamed of running away to the sea, away from his easy-going Pappy and most adoring Mammy, in search of his destiny.

He dreamed of stowing away on a big boat, and he did, he was a stowaway for many a day. Till he was discovered and put to work. Rubbing the floors, cleaning the galley, it just wasn't up his alley.

He began to dream of an island where he could live off the land and do as he pleased, and if he pleased not, not do. Strangely, his dream came true.

The ship developed some trouble and had to be docked, the boy ran away, believing the island unoccupied, next morning bid the ship goodbye from his perch on a tree. He came down to live off the land and find his destiny.

He found a family of four, who adopted him before he could say otherwise, he was asked to study harder and also do some chores.

He was the youngest. The father of the family was a very

hard-working man and that is what he taught his children. He loved them all equally and he made the work all equally, he believed in the school of life and the school of work and the school of hard knocks. The mother believed in God, cleanliness and home cooked food and not necessarily in this order. She made them pray, she made them clean, she made them cook. She was ahead of her times; gender equality and chore equality were value chapters in her book.

One night the family was celebrating the community festival and the father asked what you would like to have as a dessert.

This young boy asked for a coconut. Well, we're in luck, responded the father, for the island was a beautiful tropical paradise and it abounded in coconut trees. The whole family walked to the shore and found a coconut tree. It was a moonlit night.

The youngest of the young, this young boy was to climb up to the top of the tree to acquire the coveted coconut. For the father believed that all the sweet things that we desire in life must be worked for and aspired for.

The waves are doing their job.

The moon is doing its job.

The stars are doing their job.

The trees are doing their job.

Everyone does their job.

That's how the world works.

You must do your job.

He climbed up.

The first step up took away his hesitation.

The second step up took away his consternation.

The third step up took away his fear.

The fourth step up took away his comfort.

The fifth step up brought forth determination.

He was halfway up before he thought where he was.

He had wanted to run from his destiny.

Had he already been hunted down by his destiny?

It was a small island community of folks given to hard work and piety. Was this his destiny? "The human beings propose, the will of the universe does dispose."

"That's a strange story. You should not be telling such a story. You are a star. You should tell motivating stories. You are famous, if you tell such things, people will be discouraged. I am not a famous man, I am a grocer, but I will tell you about me," so said Daanish, the grocer, to Zen the movie star.

Everything that goes around, comes around, and brings along a bagful of the same.

XI.

The Grocer's Tale

"My mother was an addict; I never knew my father. I grew up on the streets, with life's knocks and kicks. Scrounging for food, searching for shelter, I learnt to read in a pavement shack, sleeping on the street, beside a shack. I worked, did not beg, kept myself as clean as I could, in a place where it was difficult to keep a shirt on my back.

I learned a few words of English, French, Italian and such. I began to offer help, often and much. The railway station and the guest houses I haunted, the tourists, the travellers, I could get them anything they asked for and wanted. My dream was to own a grocery store of my own."

"As you do now."

"Yes. And I am happy."

"Good for you."

"I did not just want to earn. I wanted to create something of value."

"And a grocery store is your something of value?"

"Do you know it is food that nourishes you and keeps you in good health. Everything I sell is of the best quality available, each and everything. And the staples are always marked down, so that everyone can buy. I have gone hungry many a times, I know starvation. And my regulars, they always pay forward for the meals of the poor, it's a celebration of food, and all things good. I know it is just a neighbourhood grocery store, but it creates value every day."

He paused contemplating value.

"My dream was to make sure that families that barely survive, can keep body and soul alive. I sell cakes that an old lady bakes, wholesome respect it takes. She will not take charity for she has her cakes, and her kitchen is her bakery. During the lockdown, I hung two baskets out of the store, one with bread, the other with a jar. Those who needed bread took them, those who could pay, put the money in the jar."

"Did you make money or lose it?"

"None, my friend, no one in the neighbourhood went to bed hungry, and we broke even. And once things were better, the jar filled up faster and faster."

Ben jumped up and hugged Daanish. "I will always shop with you."

Be mindful of that jar, I said.

"Daanish's Greens and Garnishes."

He glowed like an apple.

"I am happy. Dreams should make us happy."

Tara clapped her hands in delight, "I will tell your story to my kids. You bring light."

The good doctor stepped out of his sleepless slumber to say, "Bravo!"

The stockbroker drawled, "I bet the jar went laughing to the bank."

The apple was blushing.

"I do not question your intentions; I evaluate the outcome of your actions. When there is blood on the streets, someone makes money. Rothschild said buy when there is blood on the streets."

He continued, addressing himself to the good doctor, "Mr Opar Chewn, you were almost assaulting, and here you are cheerfully applauding. Sir, may I inform you that both took up the opportunity and made good of it. May I seek to question you a bit?"

The good doctor looked tired and sighed, "I have seen folks die."

Haggard, he closed his eyes.

Money is important. But money alone is not wealth. Wealth is more than money. Wealth is more important than money.

Create wealth rather than money.

A rich man may not be a wealthy man, but a wealthy man is always rich.

XII.

The Industrialist's Tale

The industrialist spoke, "We are the Pauls. Paul Brothers Incorporated. You might have heard of our business and wealth accumulated."

We were all suitably impressed.

Let me tell you a real story. A real story from the real world. I am a real man and a man of the world, as Philippe de Rothschild was a real man and a man for the world.

During World War II, he was enlisted to serve in the French Air Force. The quick fall of France resulted in de Rothschild being arrested in Algeria by the Vichy government and the vineyard property seized.

His French citizenship was revoked on 6 September 1940. Released from Vichy custody in April 1941, Philippe de Rothschild made his way to England, where he joined the Free French Forces of General Charles de Gaulle, earning a Croix de Guerre medal. After the Allies' liberation, Philippe de Rothschild learned that, although his daughter was safe, the Gestapo had, on charges of attempting to cross a line of demarcation with a forged permit, deported his estranged wife in 1941 to Ravensbrück concentration camp where she died; the cause of her death remains unknown to date. She died in the Holocaust, that's all that can be said.

The war was then over. He could give his attention back to the world and his life. The vineyard had been used unkindly by the German forces. Devastated, Rothschild turned his attention to the vineyard.

The German army had inflicted extreme damage to Chateau Mouton Rothschild. Now, he could have been devastated, like his estate was and given it up as hopeless. But what did he do? He gathered his resolve and put all his effort and determination into restoring the vineyard and by the early 1950s was once again producing wine.

Not only producing wine again, he put it on the wine map of the world as one of the premier wines that exists today. Herein lies the indomitable spirit of human achievement. When he returned, the prisoners of war were encamped all over his estate. He fed them well, treated them well, but put them to work to rebuild the buildings and the structures. Here lies enterprise and learning.

It was a good story. The Paul brothers were all about expensive colognes, impressive chronometers, and rich leather, the birds of an elite feather.

Spooney sidled up to them, "Sir, if you have some spare time today?"

The manicured hand waved him away. Without looking up from his screen, he took a moment to say, "Buy. Tech, pharma, or infra."

The Goth punk rocker Ivy began to jump on her seat, screaming at the top of her voice, “Capitalists are bastards! Selling our planet!”

The band screamed back, “Hell! Yeah!”

The gentleman looked at her with one eyebrow raised and asked, “Selling to whom, young lady?”

“Don’t tell me you don’t know!”

“I don’t know.”

“Capitalists selling to capitalists.”

“Hell! Yeah!” screamed the band.

Love is a true myth.

Love is a mythical truth.

Or just an oxymoron in itself.

XIII.

The Sailor's Tale

A few of us were already dreaming of a rich strike. The sailing man shrugged as if it wasn't much of a concept to like. Sunny the sailor seemed scorched by the sun, drowned in clouds, of sadness and an undefinable sorrow, he did not believe in a beautiful tomorrow.

"Money is just money, but you need love. Real love, true love. When I was a boy, I had read Homer's Odyssey, in translation, of course, for Greek was Greek to me, but even as a boy I wanted a life on the sea, I wanted to sail and be free.

But love, and love that is loyalty is even more liberating than the sea. Do you remember Penelope? My friend, do you remember her? Her eyes are deeper, her heart truer than the wine-dark sea. Do you remember Penelope? She weaves by the day, she unravels by night, she smiles in the day, she cries all night, her tears fall free. Do you remember Penelope? You left her alone in the city of stone, for you the world, for her the hearth, she waits with abiding love and loving loyalty. Do you remember Penelope? The suitors are around, the troubles escalate, the obstacles abound, she does not forget even for a moment, her man facing the might of the sea. Do you remember Penelope? The call of adventure, the call of your king, the call of your mates, the call of the siren, for you and your wanderings, the call of the sea.

"Do you remember Penelope?"

There was depth in his words, and a deeply felt pain, deeper than the fathomless sea.

I am glad that he is not driving this bus because he is surely under the influence. Isn't that such a cliche, this drunk sailor, unhappy, moving ahead with no direction, living and yet not alive, a ghost of his former life?

His heart is broken, and you can see it.

You can see that his path is one of misery, and there is no mending it.

His will has been overcome by another, and there is no defending it.

His heart is broken, and he can see it too.

"Penelope!"

He cried. And slid into his senseless stupor.

Step into the story you are told.

Find the other side.

Listen.

All is revealed if you listen.

XIV.

The Escort's Tale

The woman who had agreed to sing for supper or more seemed quite shaken to her core.

She spoke in an untutored diction,

True love is all poetry and fiction.

People judge you; lovers leave you; friends backstab you; husbands deceive you.

Villains who live and die defamed have been misjudged and renamed, like the Queen offered an apple to Snow White, but no one ever listened to her. Right?"

The Duo Magnifico, Kai and Zen, were listening with attention.

"I am Rosa, and I felt it in my heart, maybe these are the words that the Queen said to Snow White...

My heart, my heart, the apple is to set you free to wander forever far and beyond, in the everlands and the Neverland, in the morning mists and evening haze, in the clouds and the sky, in the curve of a smile, in the twinkle of an eye, in the lands of ecstasy and the seas of eternity, in dreams deeper than the living world's, in a living that's truer than this sleeping earth.

My heart, my heart, even princesses married to stodgy sensible princes are caught in the web of monotony, the courtesy of the court, the conduct of those who bear to bear you, surrounded by the fake and the fabulous who envy and fear you. The dull are dull, the dull are dull tales of dull matrimony. You were meant for dreamings, wanderings, excitement and happenings, and many indescribable magnificent things.

"My heart, my heart, had you bitten into this luscious flesh with love, it would not be a sin. For sin is but a perspective, a privilege, and a prerogative, that too not of a perfect heart, for no heart is perfect within. Love changes all to love, love lives with love, when you live with love.

Had you bitten the core with courage and conviction, it would have flown you far from the mundane and mal-intention. It would have been a ladder to the stars through the steps chiselled out of the sky, the stars below the infinity above. My heart, my heart, wronged were you, and wronged was I, by all those who told my story, for no story is ever told in all its telling, and therein lies the devil.

Trust no tales that speak of good or evil.

Whose story is the story?

Who is doing the telling?

Who is listening?

My heart, my heart, trust your heart."

Rosa spoke with passion and was correct after a fashion. Do we really listen to the other side, or jump to our conclusions with prejudiced haste? It was a good question that brought to mind a confusion. Was she against love or did she seek it out of desperation?

Love is a journey, love is a destination, love is a person, love is an emotion, love is a bond, love is the only reality, love is beautiful, and love is everything, for some of us.

The others will remain untouched by love.

Yet both will find happiness.

XV.

The Other Actor's Tale

Kai, spirited and lively, oozing charm and theatre began speaking in a voice one would listen to all of a lifetime and beyond.

"Ribbons and frills, pretty pink dresses, froth and lace

Not me!! Torn denims, worn sneakers, a soccer-streaked face.

Untidy! Grew up wild, wild hair, a wilder head, the wildest by far.

Dance all night, laugh in the bar, drink with the mates, born under a crazy star.

Dance with queens, lose my losses, love my loves, bear my crosses.

Order in my disorder, disorder in my order, a madness in my method, a method in my madness.

Call me by my name or call me a hot mess.

Or call me the devil walking in a red dress.

I am Kai,

I will tell you a story, it is one that the bard told. (She was exuding devotion, as she spoke of The Bard, she was overwhelmed by emotion)

There is no story like this story."

She climbed on a seat, threw her strong theatre voice till it travelled from our ears directly to our hearts.

"It is a tale of love, for I believe in love. True love. Juliet and Romeo

loved, a long time ago

star crossed destiny tossed

coming from families that hated each other

A hate that was forever.

They won't be allowed to marry it's avowed.

Ah! Star-crossed storm-tossed

Like riders in the storm, in spirit and form.

Death marks tragedy dark.

Just before the wedding night, the family, to fire-heaping fuel,

Romeo kills her cousin in a duel.

The morning after, forced to leave without her. Romeo returns to the city. Death awaits!

An atrocity, marry another, marry Paris today!

Her parents did not know. she had married some time ago, she plans to die, in fact, fake it.

Romeo dies for love's sake. Love forever, die together. Star crossed, tragedy tossed."

What are we if we do not truly love? I have a heart; I have a soul.

I have a mind, I have a body, I have emotions and needs.

I will have a true partner who must respect me, who will stand by me, who will live with me, who will be with me.

They could not live together but they could die together.

Death is not the answer, but what is life, if not death, if it's not fulfilled.

There is no fulfilment but love. Nothing less will satisfy your soul and your loving heart.

I believe my soulmate is waiting for me somewhere in the world.

Someday we'll be together.

The shifting light danced across her bright blindness and uber-gorgeousness.

Some of us broke out in applause.

The lawyer didn't applaud. She looked quite cross. She looked like a storm meeting thunder. What's her story? I began to wonder, just then she shouted quite loud.

"What is so great about dying together? Or living together?

And what need does Juliet have to be married?"

Put the wet towels in the laundry basket.

Pick up after you. Respect her time.

Express your appreciation.

In multiple ways.

From time to time.

Or else.

XVI.

The Lawyer's Tale

The lawyer, much married, asserted herself in a manner unhurried.

"Love is too overrated, and to be married to one you love and live happily ever after, or to die together and find an eternal hereafter.

Perfection does not exist, stop looking for it. A woman must learn to love herself and be true. For your perfection is in your heart, and your love is within you.

A suspended moment in time and space, in my imagination exists a marvellous place. The queen does await, by the castle gate, an equal rights knight without a shining armour and a single doubt. To be rescued? Possibly not.

Out of the patriarchal rot, to find herself a living sovereign. She is that regardless of her suffering and pain. The world thrusts upon her, the dragon, the devil, the monster. She is her own comfort, her shelter, her respite, her salvation, her courage, her light.

She is not waiting for any rescuing knight, tonight or any other night, for she is her own knight.

In my imagination exists a marvellous place. The queen does not await, by the castle gate, a loving knight with a shining armour and without a doubt. To be wooed and married?

Possibly not. Out of the marital rot, to find herself totally and completely sovereign.

She is that regardless of her suffering and pain. The world thrusts upon her, the wooer, the lover, the master. She has to be her own comfort, her shelter, her respite, her salvation, her courage, her light.

She refuses to be rescued by a husband, a lover, or a knight, tonight or any other night, for she must learn to be her own knight."

Her husband looked at her in surprise, a software guy nerdy and nice.

"Whoa! Anise Discord, that's strong. I didn't know you felt like this."

"Well, now you do."

"Yes. Now I do. Are you happy with me?"

It did not seem that an answer was forthcoming.

"So much hot air! I need a drink!" exclaimed Tau, the pharmacist.

Rosa offered to share some, "I have some cheap wine off the rack." Sunny the sailor spoke from somewhere at the back.

"Come join me. I have a dozen, from here to doom." Tau and Rosa joined him, ready to consume."

"Hot air! What are you implying?" Anise spoke with an underlying bitterness.

History has always been a lesson.
Humanity does not like lessons.
Until it is taught a lesson.
Liking it doesn't matter then.

XVII.

The Pharmacist's Tale

"Madam, all respect to you, but do you know there are people dying?

To love, to have loved, to forget, seems your only regret.

I have been working all hours, keeping the pharmacy open all alone, people asking for medicines and there are none.

It has been a battle all uphill, with rocks rolling downhill, taking a toll."

Anise retorted sharply, "And all you do as people get sicker, meet your mates to consume liquor?"

Tau spoke in a deep baritone; he told us about times long gone.

"Let me tell you about the Spanish flu. Europe in Nineteen Eighteen. Wave after wave after wave came in.

A mild first one in the spring, in winter the next and most devastating, and the last moderate one in early 1919.

In the beginning and for many months to pass, it was not recognized as a major threat that it was.

In July of 1918, it was still being compared to previous flu outbreaks in former years, with that of the last pandemic, it quelled peoples' fears.

The tone of physicians remained moderate and anti-alarmist throughout the Pandemic which would prove to be the most catastrophic.

Society faced challenges not unlike our own, economic disruption, crowded public transportation as people worked and partied in continuation, and having to carry out disinfection.

People died. In hospitals, in hospices, in homes, death assumes many guises. The Spanish flu was one for sure. There was no cure.

The only thing was to reduce fever, close all places of congregation, wear the mask to be followed as a religion, or a fashion, social distancing and stay in shelter. Venturing out was risky. Only two things saved life, they were indisputably oxygen and whisky.

So, Madam do not cast aspersions due to your ignorance, on the precious waters of life that brought deliverance and give us sustenance."

Ali laughed and exclaimed, "Hear! Hear!" The band broke into a college drinking chant, "Drink, drink, drink. Hell Yeah."

Are you reading between the lines?
Always do so, that's where the meaning hides.

XVIII.

The Doctor's Tale

"One fact I do agree with is that we should have learned our lessons, from history, from medicine, to lessen the number of fatalities. We could have improved our functionality. We could have been prepared better and worked smarter."

His tone was philosophical.

"Let me tell a tale. It is a folk tale. In a forest, a world of green, there lived a tribe of big people and another of the little people, who were neither heard nor seen. The little people could see each other but could never work together. The big ones were called Bigheads, the little ones were called Littlefeet. The Bigheads knew all about the Littlefeet but did not pay them much attention. They were never seen, heard or considered a valuable population.

The Bigheads constructed skyways to constellations and mansions that defied imagination. The Littlefeet gathered fruit and baked bricks, simple folk, no treats no tricks."

The good doctor continued with his narration.

Then something terrible began to take place, the trees

began to wither and shrivel and collapse, the trees were no greener, some would crash, some would burn in a flash. No trees, no food, no houses, no skyways, cold nights and hungry days. Bigheads blamed Littlefeet, who blamed Bigheads, who blamed Littlefeet. No one was wrong and no one was right, it was a fierce fight with no end in sight.

Things turned from bad to worse, a catastrophe, a calamity, a curse. Some wise persons came up with an advisory, some horticulturists discussed a cure, some arboriculturists suggested a procedure, anything could be tried though nothing was sure. It required some refined stardust and diamond-bladed knives to slice heavenly fruit, the core was to be mixed with stardust and fed to the innermost part of the root.

(The roots are important, they should always be protected, with strong roots, the stems and leaves can grow as expected.) With human hands at the incidence of the first ray of the sun. The Bigheads had all of it at their disposal, but their stature was such that they could not reach them, so forwarded a proposal.

The Littlefeet should do it, Bigheads would get all provisions. To survive, both tribes needed to exist in cooperation. In mutuality in harmony in goodwill, there is benefit. In coordination and cooperation, there is mutual profit.

Bigheads and Littlefeet designed a policy new, to live in harmony, the trees stopped collapsing and grew. Bigheads realized that Littlefeet were people too. They had never given them a listening; they had never been heard. The Bigheads changed their ways, coexistence was the word.

There was no more an 'us and them', it was always 'we', peace, progress and a flowering, flourishing forest was how things were meant to be.

Always listen to good advice.

Or don’t. It’s your life.

XIX.

The Ambulance Driver's Tale

The ambulance driver retorted looking cross.

"Things are never as they are meant to be."

He continued in a sharp tone, "That's like you imagine utopia and exist day after day in dystopia. And no one asks how you are, and how was your day, and if they ask, they don't want to know for they have themselves had a tough day.

Each day is worse than the last, the future is bleaker than the past."

The band screamed, "There is no tomorrow, for it is dead."

I asked him to introduce himself and tell his story.

This is what he said.

"My name is Justin Time and I work in the City Hospital as an ambulance driver. For the last twenty-five years, I have been doing my best to save lives, in my own way, this year I failed many times."

He seemed disturbed yet went on, "There is an island in the middle of the sea, the sea is turbulent and scary, the waves are taller than the ships they carry, but no ships are seen, for the sailors are wary, there are ships and secrets and bodies buried deep, the sea captures them forever to keep.

One young man, ambitious and impulsive, said the world he wished to explore, the island is not my everything, life must give me more. All the islanders, learned and wise, gathered around him to offer advice.

'Build a boat extremely strong.'

'Practice your strokes day and night long.'

'Learn patience, improve skill.'

'Talk to the waves, build goodwill.'

'Prepare in detail a plan B.'

'Don't embark on your journey till you are ready.'

'Don't make any decisions while being hasty.'

Being young, ambitious and arrogant, he thought all advice was abhorrent. He knew he was ready to go, he knew all that there was to know. He put out his boat, he put up his sail, he rode the waves, he rode them right into the pale.

The stormy ocean is the world we are in, the boat is the self, packaged with skills and competency, trained to exert with learning and proficiency. Our fears are the demons in the storms, our demons take many forms. The journey is this journey, stormy is the world's sea. He threw in his lot to sink or swim, to fail or win, to live or die, without giving himself a real chance. The boat capsized in the deadly dance, of the waves of adversity that suffered no pain. That particular young man was never seen again.

“I don’t like this narrative, it is neither poetic nor creative,” the undergraduate, Kale objected. “It’s too much of dos and don’ts, like the stuff to which we have been subjected. No parties, no classes, no contact sports, no wild dates. I am sick of this. Do you know how long it’s been since I have been to a pub or had a hug and a kiss? I tell you, I am sick of this. I am bored. I stare at my screen, my cell. This is dumb as hell. There is no excitement, there is no adventure. I feel old, no bite, no teeth, no denture. What is life without fun?”

“Would you like to tell us a story?”

“No. And I don’t want to listen to y’all either. Blah, blah!”

That seemed final.

The truth has many faces, some seen others
unseen, some that could have been

One for the lost and lonely, one for those torn
stumbling in the dark, one for those who have no
words, no voice, just a soul shredded to
nothingness

One for power, one for might, another for the
devil within, one for those prowling on the street,
one you smile at, another you would be afraid to
meet, in the darkened corner of your room, on
the darkest night

One you show to the world, one you store hidden
from all eyes, one you choose to meet in the
mirror, one you can only deny.
One that resembles itself, but barely,
another you buried alive.

XX.

The News Anchor's Tale

The news anchor asserted, "Let me tell you one. My name is Sky. You might have seen me. You might know my name; I have had my share of popularity and fame. In the world of news, I am a star, you might wonder how it came about. Well, it was the Gulf War. I think all stories are very important, they are about incidents and bring out a viewpoint, the outlook may broaden and impact the audience's standpoint. I sell stories, I tell them good, they are my identity, my livelihood. Some of you might remember the Gulf War."

The FourForFour erupted with "Down with war! Down with brutality. Down with war! It's against humanity!"

Sky did not falter for a bit; he kept on right at it. "There were hundreds of channels, thousands of reporters, CNN was already doing live coverage, television, print, sound and image. Pro-war—anti-war and all shades in between. The general, with many coup attempts and soldiers' execution, ruled from 1979, till his overthrow by a US-led coalition. The war reporting was sensational, the players international, the vested interests gigantic, then the focus on weapons of mass destruction.

My focus was on stories of human interest, the real devastation. Melancholy, mourning, heartache, deaths, grief, heartbreak, the poignant hopelessness, anguished despair."

"Even in suffering, the vultures do not spare the living!" Kale was aggravated.

Sky waved his hands expressively. "How do the powerless tell their stories so far untold?"

"For vultures like you, sorrow and suffering is gold."

"It is all about perspective, everything is relative and respective, to the incident, the accident, the happening, the mishappening."

"What about the truth? Your truth? The truth of the news you report?"

"Truth is incidental, sometimes accidental. It changes form to find multiple views. I am your Man for News. Reporter for the Gods. Or almost gods! Those who make this world go, on whom the world turns, turn to me."

"For news?" He laughed loud.

"For feeding it to simpletons like you, morons who believe in unreal words living in illusory worlds, for distortions, simulations, necessary manipulations. The individuals who consume stories and lies are deaf and blind, hear and see what we want them to, live in the world we control, the Gods and I!

People like you who cannot think individually."

"Unreal words?" He smirked.

"Fair play, justice, equality, and truth."

Allow light to enter your being.

Rather welcome it.

XXI.

The Man of God's Tale

"I am reminded of a story, if I have your permission." His voice was as warm and compassionate as his demeanour.

"Please, sir."

"Please call me Viktor. The tale I wish to tell is about a great master. This great master was once walking with three acolytes, by a riverbank. They asked him, 'O Great Master, tell us, what is the truth of life?'

He invited each of the acolytes to describe two things they could hear, two things in their sight, and the one in their heart and mind.

The first one spoke thus, 'Master, I see the young children playing on the riverbank, and the young couples walking around with much love in their eyes and gestures. I hear the laughter of the young children and the soft chatter of those in love.

I feel their happiness, in their play, in their laughter, in their conversations. There is joy in their actions and words.'

The second one spoke thus, ‘Master, I see the beautiful colours of the setting sun reflected in the enchanting river. I see the magnificent trees providing solace and shade by the riverbank. I hear the boatmen’s song and the chirping of the birds.

I am filled with appreciation, towards the glory of natural beauty and the bounty of nature.’

The third one spoke thus, ‘Master, I see the eternal immensity of the sky. I see the peaceful depth of the river. I hear the chanting of the wind and the meditation of the water.

I am filled with gratitude, that I have been given the gift of life to be a part of this vastness, that I can be impacted so deeply by beautiful images and sounds, that I can enjoy all this and everything that life offers.’

The master laughed and said, ‘This is the truth of life. The happiness of being with other humans, appreciation of all that is worthy, and gratitude for everything that we have.’

The master told them to go on their own journeys for they knew the right question to ask, and they had vision. One must have sight, and one must have vision, for that leads to wisdom, which leads to knowledge.”

There was silence, maybe everyone was napping, or they were contemplating, till one strong and deep voice broke the silence.

“There is one more truth. Or just one truth.”

It was the grave digger.

All journeys are marked by their destinations.

Life is a journey.

XII.

The Grave Digger's Tale

"My name is Maximus Reaper. You can call me Max.

This year has been the most unforgiving. I have met more deceased than the living. I spent relentless nights surrounded by coffins. My eyes grim, my resolution wearing thin.

Our friend Viktor did not disclose the fourth truth of life, the final truth, do not doubt it, yet wonder why it is we don't speak about it. Let me tell you a tale, unvarnished and true, it is not a pretty tale, it may disturb you.

The protagonist is Leo, though he is no hero. He is a regular guy, a family man much in love with his beautiful life. A beautiful home in the better part of town, a large family, a lovely loving wife. Two point five kids, dogs and pals, high on vibes, high on morale.

A sister and a brother, a father and a mother, annual vacations, weekends, get-togethers. He loved his family, a hands-on father, a real dad, a loving son, a doting husband, never letting down the kids and making them sad. He did more than anyone ever did for his kids, except for their homework assignment, though he helped them with his time and was content.

When they were little mites, he changed them and fed them even at midnight with cooing sounds and a real delight. He never forgot a birthday or an anniversary, he celebrated the little and big joys and took real pleasure in his family.

Time passed; the kids were young no longer, but the bond was stronger. For he loved them so, more than even he could know. Then came the fever and it raged, a dry cough that would not go away, a bone-deep tiredness, pains and aches, he lost his taste and sense of smell, he did not feel he was getting well. The pressure built on his chest, he could not breathe anymore, his oxygen level dipped and dipped, and dipped some more. He gasped for breath. It was his final truth.

Death.

Yet his spirit did not believe, his children and wife, he did beseech, not to let him go, or to go with him, the tunnel grew dark, the lights grew dim.

Leo held his wife in his lifeless arms, he hugged his children as he cried, they were nowhere near, it was in an isolation facility that he had died.

Brought to me in an unmarked shroud, the dying sun, the coffin a dark cloud, his spirit yet screamed and screamed so loud.

His much-loved wife was not near, his much-loved children, the contamination a contagious fear.

He had lost everything with his last breath.

He was alone, alone with death. His voice was unheard,

lost was his word.

What will you do with my soul?

With nothing, I can pay you.

I was buried in the dead of night, not a coin placed on my lids, not a loved one by my side

Son of Erebus and Nyx, do not take me across the Styx, let me not go alone, let the raft be tied, for if my loved ones are with me, my spirit can be revived, let me not be alone.

I had faith and love, let me not be denied.

I buried him in the dead of the night.

I, all by myself, and he, all by himself.

My hands have buried many, and each grave holds just one.

My eyes cry to see souls suffer and die

No oxygen, they struggle for breath

No meds, no beds, the disease spreads, in a strange eerie rampage of death.

In ordinary places burning pyres, the oath of Hippocrates screams in pain, tires, bows out, and leaves in its wake, wakes and prayer meetings for those departed, those who are living live in threat, there isn't a nightmare they haven't lived awake, wake them up or they wake up in dread.

The orphaned children still and silent, stare at nothing. For there is nothing to see, nothing to wait for, nothing to wake for.

For nothing is promised. No one is spared. Mortality has defined our final fate; death is the fourth and the final truth.

This is the one and only truth."

Max had come to the end of his tale, and we had reached our designated destination.

Whose tale was the worthiest of being told, that would be our next deliberation.

So, tell me, my friend,

whose tale was the worthiest of all?

There is no wisdom in life except the living of it.

Your decisions are your actions,
and your actions have outcomes.

Yet you are more than those outcomes.
You have power.

Your power lives in the telling of your story,
your power lives in the living of your story.

Your life is the story you tell yourself.
Your story is the life you live.

Tell it your way, because that is the only way.
Own it, or lose it forever.

Here is to a magical story!
Your story.

ACKNOWLEDGEMENTS

If it were not for Dhirendra Nath Dixit who asks me everyday if I am working on my book, if it were not for Siddhant who always expects me to do the right thing, if it were not for Suvin who always has a beautiful smile for me, if it were not for Dimple who is my moral compass, if it were not for Naresh who believes everything is possible with the right attitude, if it were not for Sameer who always has my back no matter what, if it were not for Rakesh bhaiya who keeps me supplied with endless cups of coffee, if it were not for Gizmo, the lazy lab who brings me a cuddle, none of this would be possible.

If it were not for Dr Vandana Jain who is simply phenomenal, if it were not for Bhavini who is truly inspirational, if it were not for Dipika who keeps me grounded, if it was not for Pooja who is beautiful inside out, if it were not for Neha who is a force to reckon with, if it for not for Veronica who is my soul sister, if it were not for Indrani who keeps me sane, if it were not for Monica who is absolutely incredible, if it were not for Shweta and her positive affirmations, if it were not for Smita who never fails to inspire me, if it were not for Sadhana who is my guiding light, this book would never have seen the light of the day.

If it were not for Sidharth whose presence is priceless, if it were not for Megh who listens to all my stories with enthusiasm, if it were not for Shaily whose support makes all the difference, if it were not for Ashwini who is my rock when the sea is stormy, if it were not for Manu who adds happiness to all days, this would not have been possible.

I owe gratitude to Anush Goel, Uma Bokil and the team at Inkfeathers Publishing, for being such an important part of this book, and for the painstaking attention to detail and constant striving for excellence. I am thankful to all of the Mira family for being who they are, a collective of thinking minds and loving hearts.

I owe a debt of gratitude to the vast ocean of literature that has sustained me all through my journey.

I am truly blessed to have each of you in my corner, and I look forward to continuing to learn and grow with your support.

With heartfelt gratitude,

Meeta Khanna

ABOUT THE AUTHOR

Meet Meeta Khanna, a passionate soul deeply entwined with the enchanting world of literature. Hailing from the vibrant city of New Delhi, Meeta's love for language and storytelling led her to embark on a journey of studying English literature. Along this path, she not only became a poet and a teacher but also discovered her profound connection with the written word.

With an insatiable thirst for knowledge, Meeta is a voracious reader, eagerly delving into diverse literary realms. Additionally, her wanderlust spirit has taken her on remarkable adventures, enriching her perspective and instilling a profound understanding of life's intricacies.

Through her writings, Meeta unveils a unique and delicate lens through which she observes the world. Her words are imbued with rare sensitivity and keen insight, gracefully capturing the essence of human emotions and experiences. Each piece of her work reflects the tapestry of her life, woven intricately with the threads of her personal encounters and discoveries.

Readers from all walks of life find resonance in Meeta's writing, as it transcends boundaries and speaks to the core of the human experience. Her collection of poetry, titled "Voices in My Head," showcases her expressive prowess, while her contributions to various anthologies such as "Heavy Lies the Crown," "Moment in Love," and "Poetry 365" demonstrate the breadth of her creative talent.

Meeta Khanna's penmanship beautifully portrays the myriad shades of existence, leaving an indelible mark on those who embark on a literary journey with her. As she continues to explore the world through her pen, readers eagerly anticipate the profound revelations and heartfelt stories that await them in her future works.

www.ingramcontent.com/pod-product-compliance
Lightning Source LLC
LaVergne TN
LVHW012111160826
845678LV00014B/3044

* 9 7 8 8 1 9 6 0 8 9 5 5 9 *